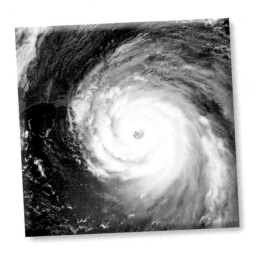

Published in 2014 by The Rosen Publishing Group, Inc.
29 East 21st Street, New York, NY 10010

Photo Credits: **KEY** tl=top left; tc=top center; tr=top right; cl=center left; c=center; cr=center right; bl=bottom left; br=bottom right; bg=background

CBCD = Corbis PhotoDisc; CBT = Corbis; DSCD = Digital Stock; GI = Getty Images; iS = istockphoto.com; N = NASA; NGS = National Geographic Society; SH = Shutterstock

**Cover** GI; **1**c N; **6**cr SH; **7**cl SH; **8**cl SH; **10**bl NGS; **12**bl, br N; **12–13**bg CBCD; **13**bl, br N; **14**cl CBT; tc GI; **16**cl DSCD; **18**bl, tl CBT; tl iS; **18–19**cr CBT; **21**tc CBT; **22**tr CBT; **26**tl SH; **28**br, br, br GI; bc SH; **28–29**bg CBCD; **29**tr, bl iS; tl SH; **30**br, c, cr SH; **30–31**bg SH

All illustrations copyright Weldon Owen Pty Ltd

Weldon Owen Pty Ltd
Managing Director: Kay Scarlett
Creative Director: Sue Burk
Publisher: Helen Bateman
Senior Vice President, International Sales: Stuart Laurence
Vice President Sales North America: Ellen Towell
Administration Manager, International Sales: Kristine Ravn

Publisher's Cataloging Data

Close, Edward.
Extreme weather / by Edward Close.
 p. cm. — (Discovery education: earth and space science)
Includes index.
ISBN 978-1-4777-6194-6 (library binding) — ISBN 978-1-4777-6196-0 (pbk.) —
ISBN 978-1-4777-6197-7 (6-pack)
1. Climatic extremes — Juvenile literature. 2. Weather — Juvenile literature. I. Close, Edward. II. Title.
QC981.8.C53 C55 2014
551.55—d23

CPSIA Compliance Information: Batch # W14PK2: For Further Information contact Rosen Publishing, New York, New York at 1-800-237-9932

## EARTH AND SPACE SCIENCE

# EXTREME WEATHER

EDWARD CLOSE

**PowerKiDS** press

New York

# Contents

# Forces of Nature

The weather influences how we live, what activities we do, and even what clothes we wear. The forces of nature are always influencing our weather conditions. Extreme weather can bring fierce blizzards and storms, along with flooding and lightning, or long droughts and heat waves lasting for months or years at a time.

### Hurricanes and flooding

A hurricane can cause serious flooding. Storm surges push seawater on shore, flooding towns near the coast. Heavy rains can also cause flooding in inland regions. Large areas of New Orleans, Louisiana, were flooded after Hurricane Katrina hit this region in August 2005.

### Ocean storms

Violent ocean storms often produce fierce winds that can create devastating ocean waves. The enormous force of these giant waves can destroy boats and sometimes entire coastal villages.

*More than 1,800 people were killed as a result of Hurricane Katrina. The damage was the most expensive to repair in America's history.*

## Lightning

During powerful thunderstorms, lightning strikes can occur. Lightning forms from a buildup of electrical energy within a thunderstorm cloud. Lightning can strike downward from a cloud, jump across clouds, or strike into the air from clouds.

## Tornadoes

Tornadoes are fierce, rotating columns of air that reach from the clouds to the ground. They often occur in a region known as Tornado Alley. When a tornado touches the ground it can lift up cars, trucks, and even buildings.

# Tornado Formation

Tornadoes are powerful, twisting funnels of rising wind that reach down from supercell thunderstorms and hit the ground. Some tornadoes last just a few seconds, while others may go on for more than an hour. A tornado forms when warmer, moist air mixes with colder, dry air inside the thunderstorm. A change of wind direction makes a column of air rotate and spiral toward the ground.

**INSIDE A TORNADO**

1 Warm, moist air enters the updraft over the cool air of the downdraft.

2 Part of the downdraft spirals inward.

3 The downdraft then rises on the outside of the tornado.

4 At the same time, the column of air begins to rotate from the outside.

5 Inside the tornado, air pressure is very low, causing air in the core to sink.

6 Mini tornadoes form at the base and carve their own looping path into the ground.

7 Each mini tornado circulates the perimeter of the tornado as it moves across land.

**Fierce beginnings**

Funnel clouds are rotating, cone-shaped columns of air that extend downward from the base of a thunderstorm, but do not touch the ground. Most tornadoes begin as funnel clouds, but many funnel clouds do not become tornadoes. A tornado funnel can range from as small as 9 feet (3 m) across to wider than 1 mile (1.6 km) across.

### That's Amazing!

Tornadoes move across the ground at speeds of up to 65 miles (105 km) per hour and can generate winds of up to 300 miles (480 km) per hour.

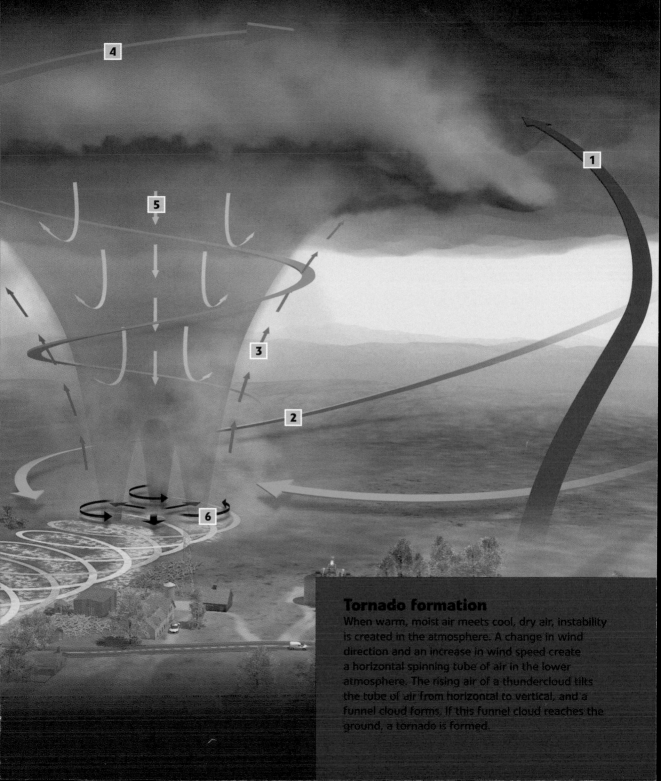

**4**

**1**

**5**

**3**

**2**

**6**

## Tornado formation

When warm, moist air meets cool, dry air, instability is created in the atmosphere. A change in wind direction and an increase in wind speed create a horizontal spinning tube of air in the lower atmosphere. The rising air of a thundercloud tilts the tube of air from horizontal to vertical, and a funnel cloud forms. If this funnel cloud reaches the ground, a tornado is formed.

# Tornado Destruction

Extensive damage occurs when a tornado touches down. Changes in wind speed and direction send the mini tornadoes inside the main funnel on a path of destruction. Most tornadoes rarely last longer than 10 minutes, but even in a small amount of time they can wreak havoc, uplifting cars and ripping roofs off buildings. Tornadoes often occur in spring when hot, dry air meets warm, moist air and kill hundreds of people each year worldwide.

## Deadly force

A tornado's powerful winds can carry massive objects for miles (km). They can uplift cars, trees, people, even entire houses, in seconds. The deadliest tornado occurred in Tornado Alley in 1925. It traveled 219 miles (353 km) and killed 695 people.

## TORNADO LOCATIONS

Tornadoes can occur across many parts of the world, but a small area in the Midwest, known as Tornado Alley, is hit by hundreds of them each year. The combination of warm, moist air and cooler, dry air results in massive supercell thunderstorms that can often lead to a tornado forming.

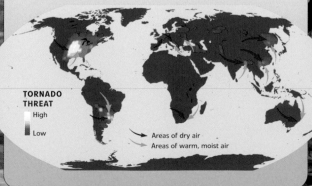

TORNADO THREAT

High

Low

→ Areas of dry air
→ Areas of warm, moist air

**Hollow tube**
Low air pressure in the center of the funnel cloud forms a calm, inner core surrounded by fierce, rotating winds. From a distance, a tornado can appear like a giant trunk or snaking rope reaching down from the sky.

# Hurricane Formation

Hurricanes are large, powerful storms that can reach 600 miles (965 km) across and can generate violent, spiraling winds of up to 200 miles (320 km) per hour. They originate over warm, tropical oceans and generally travel with the direction of the wind, bringing heavy rain and inland flooding when they reach land. Called hurricanes in the Atlantic, Caribbean, and Western Pacific, they are known as tropical cyclones in Australia and the Indian Ocean, and as typhoons in the Western Pacific.

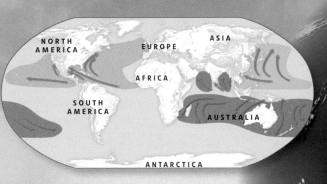

**MAP KEY**
- ☐ Typhoon
- ■ Cyclone
- ☐ Hurricane

**Hurricane movement**
Hurricanes begin in areas in tropical oceans just north and south of the equator. They travel along paths shown by the arrows above.

**Tropical disturbance**
Hurricanes often begin as clusters of clouds and thunderstorms called tropical disturbances. These low-pressure areas feature weak pressure gradients and little or no rotation.

**Tropical depression**
The thunderstorms in the disturbance release heat, which warms areas in the disturbance. The disturbance intensifies into a tropical depression, with an irregular partial ring of cloud.

**INSIDE A HURRICANE**

**1** A mature hurricane consists of bands of thunderclouds.

**2** The eye is a clear, almost calm area at the center of the storm.

**3** Bands are fed by warm, moist updrafts as they spiral toward the eye.

**4** The air is warmest and circulates fastest at the base.

**5** In the upper levels, the air spirals outward from the hurricane's center.

**6** As the hurricane approaches land, a storm surge can drive seawater deep inland.

## How a hurricane forms
The warm ocean heats the air above, increasing the level of water vapor in the air. When the moisture condenses into clouds, the air pressure drops and strong winds are created. These strong winds spin faster as they move across the ocean, and a hurricane is born.

## Hurricane formation
Wind speeds increase as cooler air rushes underneath the rising warm air and the tropical depression begins to rotate, forming a hurricane. It has deep convection, a visible eye, and spiral arms.

## Reaching land
As the hurricane reaches land, it loses its supply of warm oceanic air and begins to weaken. The difference in air pressure decreases, winds slow, rain eases, and the entire storm is tamed.

# Hurricane Destruction

Despite learning much about hurricanes, we are powerless to stop their devastating effects when they reach land. Violent winds can uproot trees and demolish buildings. Heavy rain and giant waves wash away cars, roads, and bridges. Homes can be flattened and people killed. Once a hurricane has passed, some cities are left completely destroyed.

The **Daily News**

## HURRICANE KATRINA

### New Orleans natural disaster

On August 29, 2005, New Orleans was hit by a massive hurricane that killed more than 1,800 people and became the costliest hurricane disaster in US history. The damage bill is estimated to have reached approximately $81 billion.

*Hurricane Katrina caused catastrophic flooding to much of New Orleans.*

**Cyclone Nargis**

In May 2008, tropical cyclone Nargis struck the coast of Burma (Myanmar) in the Bay of Bengal. It caused the worst natural disaster in the country's history, killing more than 138,000 people and wiping out whole townships.

### Katrina's rescue efforts

After Hurricane Katrina struck New Orleans, people were stranded in flooded neighborhoods for days and US Coast Guard helicopters had to pull people to safety. More than 12,000 people were rescued by more than 40 helicopters in the days after the hurricane.

# Lightning

Within a large cumulonimbus cloud, ice particles swirling in the stormy air cause positive and negative charges to separate. Negative charges gather near the base of the cloud, and the result is often jagged lightning strikes between clouds or to the ground. Every day there are millions of lightning strikes across the globe—more than 100 lightning strikes every second. That's a lot of electrical activity in the sky!

## Lightning encounter

Sometimes aircraft can trigger a lightning strike by flying near an already electrically charged cloud. Aircraft, such as helicopters, are mostly made from metal. When lightning strikes, electricity runs around the outside of the aircraft but the passengers inside are safe, so long as the aircraft and its electrical systems are not damaged.

**The tail**
The pointy ends of an aircraft, such as the tail, are most likely to be struck.

## Time lapse

Lightning and thunder occur at the same time, but as light travels much faster than sound, we see the flash of lightning before we hear the thunderclap. To measure how far away lightning is, count the number of seconds between the lightning flash and the thunder. Dividing that number by five gives you the distance in miles (divide by three for kilometers).

## That's Amazing!

Lightning often strikes the highest point of an object. The Empire State Building is struck by lightning approximately 100 times each year.

**Rotor blades**
These may get damaged if struck, but usually the pilot can fly to safety.

**Strike rate**
The average commercial aircraft is struck by lightning once or twice a year.

**The cabin**
From inside the aircraft, passengers see a bright flash and hear a very loud bang.

**Travel speed**
A lightning strike travels as fast as 60,000 miles (100,000 km) per second.

**Scorch marks**
The lightning strike leaves a large scorch mark at the place it strikes the aircraft.

**Electric power**
One fork of lightning carries the same charge as power to a small town for a year.

# How to Be a Storm Chaser

## STORM CHASER

To become a storm chaser, you will need:

INTERESTS: A good knowledge and understanding of science and the weather. A partner who is willing to chase storms alongside you.

EDUCATION: Take a storm spotter course to learn all about how to follow storms safely.

EQUIPMENT: A "chase vehicle" that is fitted with safety devices, radio equipment to communicate with others, and cameras to photograph and video the approaching storm.

**Chase day**
A typical chase day starts by examining weather data for potential storm activity. Chasers then drive, sometimes for hundreds of miles (km), to the region where a storm is likely to strike.

Why do people chase storms? Some storm chasers experience a close encounter with a storm and become fascinated by its power. Some are captivated by the beauty and awesome fury that nature can unleash, while others are curious about the science behind storms—how they form and behave. Storm chasers come from all walks of life, and many travel thousands of miles (km) each year hoping to capture the image of a lifetime.

**Weather balloons**
Storm chasers often release weather balloons high into the eye of a storm to collect scientific data, such as air pressure and wind speed and direction, which can be transmitted back to the ground.

## SEVERE STORM SAFETY TIPS

### HURRICANE

**Inside:** Stay away from glass windows, unplug all electrical appliances, and try to get to upper levels to avoid possible flooding. **Outside:** Seek shelter indoors on higher ground. **In a vehicle:** Drive to higher ground away from flood-prone areas.

### LIGHTNING

**Inside:** Close all windows, and unplug all electrical appliances. **Outside:** Seek shelter in a building. Avoid tall objects, crouch down in a safe place, and avoid metal objects. **In a vehicle:** Close windows and doors, and avoid parking under trees.

### TORNADO

**Inside:** Stay away from windows. **Outside:** Lie flat in a low area and cover head. **In a vehicle:** Get out. Do not try to outrun a tornado by driving away.

### FLOODING

**Inside:** Avoid low-lying buildings. **Outside:** Seek shelter on higher ground. Avoid rivers, streams, and storm drains. **In a vehicle:** If caught in rising waters, abandon vehicle and seek higher ground.

## Hurricane hunters

Hurricanes can be tracked by special aircraft that fly above the storm, at around 40,000 feet (12,000 m). Radar equipment is used to measure the size and intensity of a brewing storm, and this information is passed on to weather stations to warn nearby communities.

## Collecting data

Also called a Doppler on Wheels (DOW), this storm chase vehicle is one of several created by American atmospheric scientist and storm chaser Joshua Wurman. The Doppler radar dish scans storms to forecast their intensity and future position.

# Firestorm

Forest fires may be ignited by lightning from thunderstorms that produce little or no rain. When flames become so intense that they create and sustain their own wind system, a firestorm forms. Firestorms can spread rapidly up slopes when strong winds are channeled through narrow spaces. If it is not controlled quickly by trained firefighters, a small fire may suddenly develop into a raging inferno. Wind gusts can shift direction quickly, catching people by surprise as the flames advance faster than people can escape.

> *Rotating winds in a firestorm can act like a small tornado. These fiery updrafts, called pyronadoes, can reach high into the sky.*

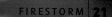

### Firefighting from the sky
Airplanes and helicopters help control fires from above by bombing them with water or chemicals. This lowers the temperature and makes trees less likely to burn.

### "Black Saturday"
In February 2009, lightning caused massive firestorms throughout forests in Victoria, Australia. Hot, gusty winds at more than 40 miles (65 km) per hour fueled the inferno, destroying hundreds of homes and farms. It is the deadliest firestorm in Australia's history. Firefighters battled the flames head on, overcoming intense heat, smoke, and ash to control the blaze.

# Hailstorm

Hail begins as tiny ice pellets, which collide with supercooled water droplets that are still liquid at temperatures below the normal freezing point. When tiny clumps of ice, kept aloft by strong winds, get blown through freezing thunderclouds, hail is formed. Updraft winds pull the hailstones up, where more droplets attach and freeze as the pellets are thrown up into freezing portions of the cloud. Once the hailstones grow too big to be kept in the air by the updraft, they fall to Earth.

**Hail damage**
Icy stones dumped from the sky can cause serious damage. Glass windows smash, and if cars are parked in the open, car hoods get badly dented.

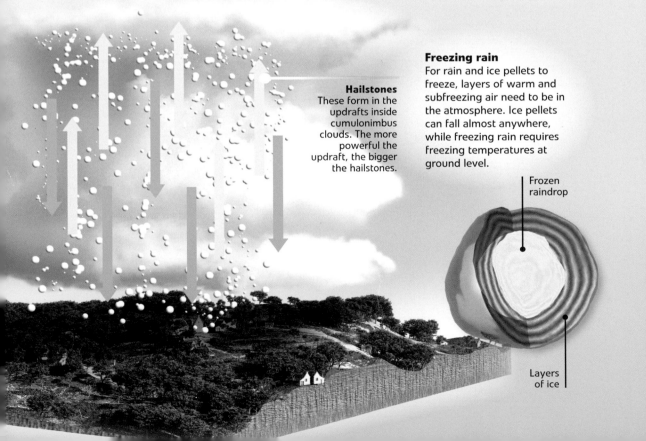

**Hailstones**
These form in the updrafts inside cumulonimbus clouds. The more powerful the updraft, the bigger the hailstones.

**Freezing rain**
For rain and ice pellets to freeze, layers of warm and subfreezing air need to be in the atmosphere. Ice pellets can fall almost anywhere, while freezing rain requires freezing temperatures at ground level.

Frozen raindrop

Layers of ice

Breaking point

# Avalanche

An avalanche is a large mass of snow and ice that slides down the slope of a mountain. Some avalanches can bury everything in their path, including trees, cars, and people. Most avalanches require three conditions to occur: an unstable snow base, a steep slope, and a trigger to kick off the avalanche. When fresh snow piles on top of base snow, the base may no longer be able to support the increased weight, and the snow base begins to slip. A small vibration, even by a skier, can trigger the avalanche.

## HOW IT HAPPENS

A slab avalanche occurs when a solid layer of snow begins to slide because of a weaker, underlying layer. Other avalanches are triggered when the snow becomes saturated with water.

Heat from the Sun

Snow

Wind

Rain

Avalanche

Slab

Ground

Weak layer

**Running to safety**
Avalanches can reach speeds of 185 miles (300 km) per hour. In 1999, an avalanche in Galtur, Austria, buried 57 people. Rescuers, using sniffer dogs, located and saved 26 trapped survivors. When an avalanche is triggered, it is best to seek shelter or move to a safe distance.

# Flood

Floods occur when too much rain, brought by sudden or continuing storms, cannot be absorbed by the soil. Rivers burst their banks, levees are broken, and water spills onto land. Strong ocean winds can also produce huge waves that flood coastal areas. When floodwaters rise slowly, people have time to move to higher ground, or build barriers to protect their homes. When water rises too quickly, they can get caught in the flood. Water damages buildings and homes, vehicles are washed away, and some people drown.

## Floods in Peru

El Niño is a climate pattern in which warm currents flow along the equator, across the Pacific Ocean to northern South America. Warmer surface water increases the number of severe storms, bringing heavy rain and flooding to Peru and Ecuador. Local agriculture and fishing industries are greatly affected.

# THAMES BARRIER

Engineers in London, UK, created giant barriers to prevent storm surges from the sea threatening the city. The Thames Barrier is a series of artificial floodgates that can be rotated upward to block floodwaters from bursting the river Thames, then rotated back downward once the surge risk has eased.

Steel-covered shell

Rocker beams

Gate

Gate arm

Potential high water level from flood surge

Barrier raised

Barrier lowered

Normal river flow

## Satellite view

This series of satellite images captures the development of El Niño. The mass of warm water (shown here as pale pink) can be seen spreading along the west coast of North, Central, and South America. A year later, current and wind conditions reversed as La Niña, a period of extensive cooling of surface water in the eastern Pacific Ocean, began.

El Niño October 1997

La Niña November 1998

Normal conditions November 2003

# Drought

A lengthy period of less than average rainfall in a particular region is called a drought. Droughts can last for months, sometimes even years. Some parts of the world experience droughts every few years. A drought means that farmers do not have enough water for crops to grow or for pastures to produce enough grass for livestock. Even native animals and plants may die of thirst.

**Beijing dust storm**
Dust storms occur when gusty winds blow loose sand and dust from a dry surface, sometimes for hundreds of miles (km). As they cross the countryside, they can appear as a solid wall 1 mile (1.6 km) high. A dust storm that hit Beijing in March 2010 created havoc for transportation systems and people.

**Disappearing streams**
Without rain, rivers and lakes can dry up and sometimes disappear completely. Even ground deep below the surface can dry out.

## DESERTIFICATION

Climate change, overgrazing, deforestation, and increased soil salinity can all degrade the land, leading to desertification. Agriculturally productive land can sometimes also turn into desert when nearby sand blows over the land. When agricultural fields are destroyed, farmers have to relocate to find more fertile soil.

**Forced migration**
Farmers abandon unproductive fields in search of more fertile land.

**Dust storm**
Winds blow sand and soil from the degraded grassland.

**Settlement in peril**
The nearby village is threatened by the moving sand.

**Dead crops**
Sand dunes gradually cover fields and crops are destroyed.

**Dust devils**
Extreme temperatures
cause fast-rising
updrafts of air. Dust is
carried into the air
and spinning "dust
devils" are created.

*Did You Know?*
When rainfall finally arrives after
years of desert conditions,
Earth's surface is too hard to
absorb the water. The result is
sudden "flash" flooding.

**Cracked earth**
After no rainfall
for years at a time,
the soil becomes
rock hard and its
surface cracks.

**All dried up**
From 1984 to 1988, Ethiopia and other parts of
Eastern Africa suffered a disastrous drought that
killed more than 1,000,000 people. Livestock had
no food or water to survive and many native
animals lost their habitat.

# Record Breakers

**2**  The Enhanced Fujita (EF) scale rates the strength of a tornado. Between 2007 and 2010, two tornadoes in the US have been rated EF5, the most devastating category.

From violent storms bringing tornadoes and hurricanes, to disastrous droughts and avalanches, the weather's destructive power can have deadly consequences. People have observed and measured extreme weather events for hundreds of years. A weather station must have 10 years of measurements before an extreme reading is considered an official record.

**8**  The Saffir–Simpson scale rates the severity of hurricanes. Between 2000 and 2009, eight Atlantic hurricanes in the US rated category 5, indicating the greatest potential damage.

**19**  The world's largest hailstone landed on June 22, 2003, in Aurora, Nebraska. It measured 19 inches (48 cm) in circumference.

**322**  Bogor in West Java, Indonesia, has recorded the world's greatest number of thunderstorm days, with an average of 322 days every year.

**409**  The village of Kifuka, in the Democratic Republic of Congo, has the most lightning strikes in the world. Its average number of strikes per square mile (ha) per year is 409.

**71.85**  The world record for the highest 24-hour precipitation is 71.85 inches (1,825 mm), which took place at Foc-Foc, Reunion Island, on January 7 and 8, 1966.

## TOP 10 STORMS

1  Bhola cyclone, Bangladesh, 1970. 500,000 deaths.

2  Hooghly River cyclone, India and Bangladesh, 1737. 350,000 deaths.

3  Haiphong typhoon, Vietnam, 1881. 300,000 deaths.

4  Coringa cyclone, India, 1839. 300,000 deaths.

5  Backerganj cyclone, Bangladesh, 1584. 200,000 deaths.

6  Great Backerganj cyclone, Bangladesh, 1876. 200,000 deaths.

7  Chittagong cyclone, Bangladesh, 1897. 175,000 deaths.

8  Super Typhoon Nina, China, 1975. 171,000 deaths.

9  Cyclone 02B, Bangladesh, 1991. 140,000 deaths.

10 Great Bombay Cyclone, India (from the Arabian Sea), 1882. 100,000 deaths.

## HURRICANES: SAFFIR–SIMPSON SCALE

|   | Wind speed, mph (km/h) | Damage |
|---|---|---|
| 1 | 74–95 (118–152) | minimal |
| 2 | 96–110 (153–176) | moderate |
| 3 | 111–130 (177–208) | extensive |
| 4 | 131–155 (209–248) | extreme |
| 5 | more than 155 (>248) | catastrophic |

This classification has been used since the 1970s to measure the intensity of a hurricane's sustained winds. It is used to estimate the potential property damage and flooding expected when a hurricane strikes.

## TORNADOES: ENHANCED FUJITA SCALE

|   | Speed, mph (km/h) | Damage |
|---|---|---|
| EF0 | 65–85 (105–137) | light |
| EF1 | 86–110 (138–177) | moderate |
| EF2 | 111–135 (178–217) | considerable |
| EF3 | 136–165 (218–266) | terrible |
| EF4 | 166–200 (267–322) | severe |
| EF5 | more than 200 (>322) | devastating |

This replaced the original Fujita scale in 2007 and rates the strength of tornadoes based on the damage they cause. The highest category, EF5, is very rare.

# Make Your Own Mini Tornado

A water vortex is a mass of fluid that forms a downward flow in the center as it moves in a circular motion. The swirling vortex draws everything it encounters toward its center. This whirlpool effect is very similar to what you see when a tornado forms.

## What you need:

☑ One large plastic bottle with cap

☑ Water

☑ Glitter

☑ Dishwashing liquid

☑ Food coloring (optional)

**1** Take the plastic bottle and remove the cap and any liquid. Fill it two thirds of the way full with water.

**2** Add a small amount of glitter to your water. Put a single drop of dishwashing liquid in the water. Put the cap back on the bottle very, very tightly.

**3** Stand the bottle upright and spin or swish it around in a circular motion, on its vertical axis, to create a tornado in a bottle.

**4** Add food coloring to the water to see your tornado even more clearly.

**5** Experiment with more or less water, or change the amount of dishwashing liquid. See if more or less water or dishwashing liquid changes your tornado formation.

**6** Try spinning or swishing the bottle more slowly or faster to see if that makes a difference.

# Glossary

**atmosphere**
(AT-muh-sfeer)
A layer of gases surrounding Earth that is held in place by Earth's gravity.

**avalanche** (A-vuh-lanch)
A sudden slide of large masses of snow down the side of a mountain.

**blizzards** (BLIH-zurdz)
Severe weather storms that produce powerful winds and heavy snow.

**cumulonimbus**
(kyoo-myuh-luh-NIM-bus)
Describes large, tall clouds that produce thunder and lightning.

**desertification**
(dih-zer-tuh-fuh-KAY-shun)
The process by which fertile land turns into barren land or desert.

**dust storm** (DUST STORM)
A severe windstorm that sweeps clouds of dust across an area.

**El Niño** (el-NEE-nyo)
A weather pattern characterized by warm ocean water in the central and eastern Pacific Ocean every three to seven years.

**Enhanced Fujita scale**
(in-HANTST FOO-jee-tuh SKAYL)
A scale used to rate the strength of tornadoes based on the damage they cause.

**firestorm** (FYR-storm)
A large, intense fire fuelled by strong gushing winds flowing in from all sides.

**flooding** (FLUD-ing)
Water that overflows onto land from rivers, lakes, or oceans, or excess surface water caused by heavy rainfall.

**hail** (HAYL)
A form of precipitation which is made up of balls or irregular lumps of ice that fall from freezing thunderclouds.

**hurricanes**
(HUR-ih-kaynz)
Large, spiraling storm systems, also known as cyclones or typhoons, which form over warm tropical oceans.

**La Niña** (lah-NEE-nya)
Opposite of El Niño, a weather pattern characterized by cooler than average ocean water in the central and eastern Pacific Ocean.

**lightning** (LYT-ning)
A sudden electrical discharge that forms from a buildup of electrical energy within a thunderstorm cloud.

**Saffir–Simpson scale**
(SAF-fur SIMP-sun SKAYL)
A scale that measures the intensity of a hurricane's sustained winds.

**satellites** (SA-tih-lyts)
Spacecraft that orbit Earth to study its surface or the weather, or to aid communication.

**storm shelters**
(STORM SHEL-turz)
Secure places built to keep people safe during wild storms.

**supercell** (SOO-pur-sel)
A large thunderstorm that is characterized by the presence of a deep, rotating updraft.

**tornadoes** (tor-NAY-dohz)
Powerful, twisting funnels of rising wind that reach down from clouds to the ground.

**tropical** (TRAH-puh-kul)
Describes warm areas of the world either side of the equator, to the north and south.

# Index

# Websites

Due to the changing nature of Internet links, PowerKids Press has developed an online list of websites related to the subject of this book. This site is updated regularly. Please use this link to access the list:

www.powerkidslinks.com/disc/extrem/